I0783121

I Love My Little Baby

Heather Lymbery

Dedication

This poem is written for my daughter, Elizabeth. It expresses a celebration of love, unity, and the joys of watching my family grow together.

I love my little baby,

It's easy as can be,

I love that little smile,

When my baby looks at me.

I love those big, bright eyes,

That tiny button nose,

The little feet that kick
And the teensy-tiny toes.

I love the little hands that reach,

For dreams I cannot see.

The hands that I will hold,

As you grow up with me.

I love the baby babble,
That will soon turn into words,

The softest little voice I know,

The cutest ever heard.

I love the sound of tiny feet
as they run across the floor.

The pitter-patter and excitement,
When there are new things to explore.

I love the little messes,
The clothes that you've outgrown.

The toys and the noise,
That makes our house a home.

I love the happy giggles,
The wiggles and the fun,

The cuddles and the snuggles
When the day is done.

And when my baby's dreaming,
In my arms, safe and warm,

I fall in love all over,
Through sunshine and through storms.

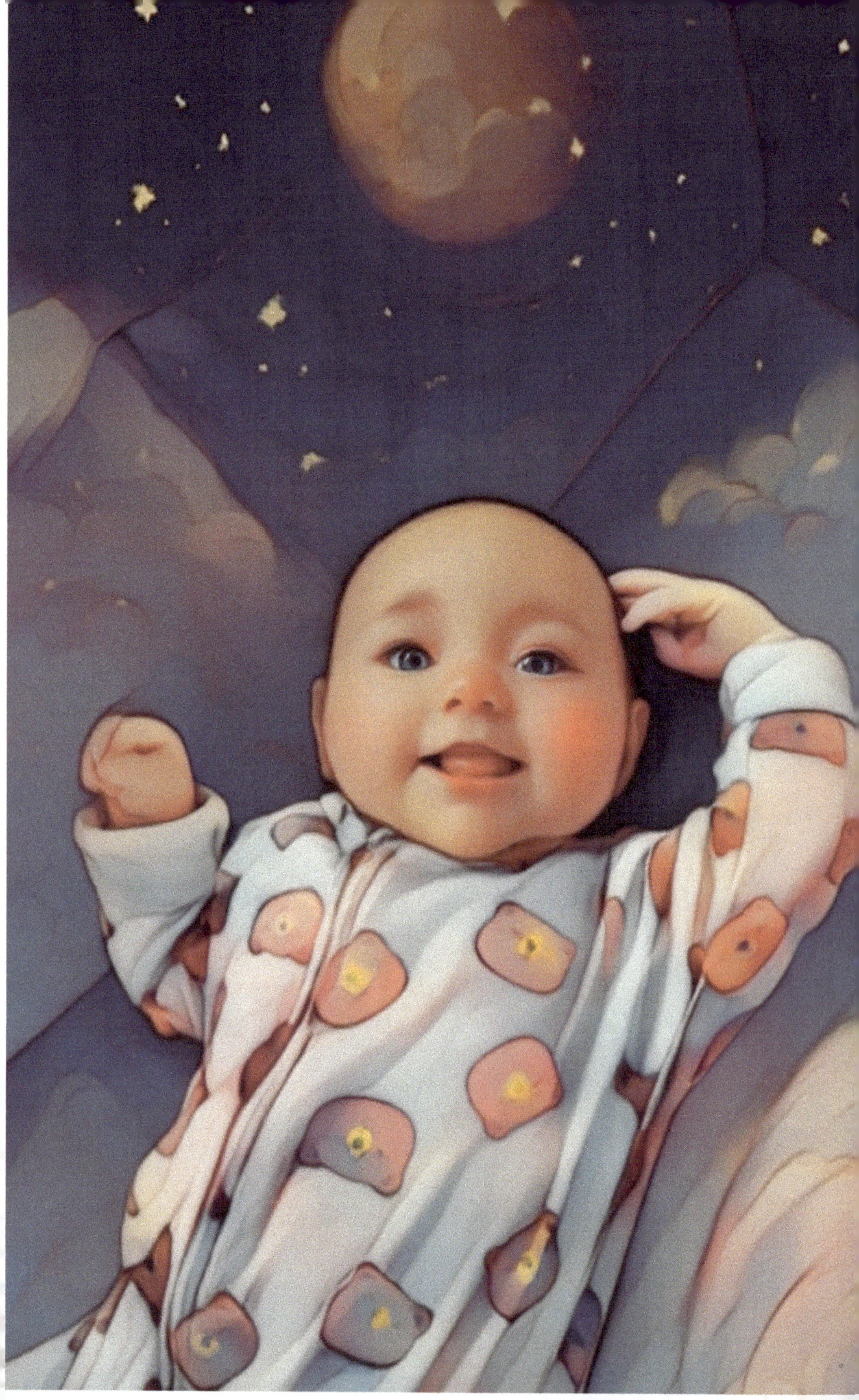

I love you, little baby,
More than words can say.

My heart will hold our memories,
When you've grown and moved away.

THE END